Baby Fozzie Visits the Doctor

By Ellen Weiss ◆ Illustrated by Tom Brannon

A GOLDEN BOOK • NEW YORK

One rainy day Baby Fozzie was in the nursery, doing a funny show for his friends, when Nanny called him.

"Fozzie," she said, "do you remember what today is? It's time to see your new doctor for a checkup."

"But I don't want to go to the doctor today,"
said Fozzie. "There's nothing funny about going
to the doctor."

"You need a checkup if you want to keep being a healthy, happy bear," said Nanny.

"Oh, all right," said Fozzie, putting on his jacket. "Bye, everybody."

In the waiting room of the doctor's office, there were colorful pictures on the walls, books to read, and even toys to play with.

Fozzie looked in a mirror—and laughed at what he saw!

A nurse opened the door. "You can come in now, Fozzie," she said.

Fozzie and Nanny followed the nurse into the examining room. "I'll wait right here," Nanny said.

"Hello, Fozzie Bear!" said the doctor. "I'm Dr. Beemer."

"Er, hi," said Fozzie.

"Now it's time to get undressed so we can weigh you and see how tall you are," said the doctor.

Fozzie got undressed and stepped onto the scale.

"You weigh 25 pounds," said Dr. Beemer. "Just about right for a bear your age. By the way, do you know where a 250-pound gorilla sits?"

"No," said Fozzie. "Where?"

"Anywhere he wants!" said the doctor.

Fozzie laughed while Dr. Beemer measured his height.

"Okay, Fozzie, now hop up onto the table for me, please," said the doctor.

Fozzie climbed up onto the big table and sat on crinkly paper.

"Now I'm going to use my stethoscope," said Dr. Beemer.

"What's a— a— stethoscope?" asked Fozzie.

"It helps me listen to your heartbeat," replied the doctor.

Dr. Beemer put the stethoscope to Fozzie's back and listened. Then he gave the stethoscope to Fozzie and said, "Now you can listen."

"It sounds like drums!" said Fozzie.

"That's why it's called your heartbeat," said Dr. Beemer.

"And now," said Dr. Beemer, "for my super-duper magic trick! Ready?"

"Ready," said Fozzie.

"Presenting," said the doctor, "my extra-special magic hammer!"

Dr. Beemer gave Fozzie's knee a little tap—
and Fozzie's leg kicked all by itself!

"Wow," said Fozzie.

"Your reflexes are working just fine," said Dr.
Beemer.

"Now," said the doctor, "please open your mouth and say 'Aaah' so that I can look down your throat."

"Aaah," said Fozzie. Dr. Beemer pressed a flat stick down on Fozzie's tongue.

"Look at that!" exclaimed the doctor. "An elephant! A big one! Other than that, your throat looks fine."

Next the doctor checked Fozzie's ears with a little flashlight.

"Good grief!" exclaimed the doctor. "A whole herd of elephants!"

"*Herd* of elephants?" echoed Fozzie.

"Of course I've heard of elephants, haven't you?" said Dr. Beemer.

"That's a good joke!" said Fozzie.

"And last," said the doctor, "we have your booster shot—to keep you from getting sick. I promise it will be over fast."

Fozzie looked away. The shot felt like a little pinprick.

"All finished!" said Dr. Beemer.

"That part wasn't so funny," said Fozzie.

"Well, maybe it wasn't," said the doctor.
"But this is." Dr. Beemer took off his glasses.
"Oh, my gosh!" exclaimed Fozzie.

"You're all finished with your checkup," said the doctor. "That means you get to pick a toy out of the prize box."

"Going to the doctor isn't so bad," said Fozzie.
"I didn't know doctors could be funny."

"Doctors are all kinds of people," said Dr.
Beemer. "I happen to be a person who likes to
make people laugh."

Fozzie couldn't wait to tell his friends about Dr. Beemer.

"I thought there couldn't be anything funny about going to the doctor," Fozzie told them.

"Boy, was I wrong!"